THE KING
WITH SIX FRIENDS

BY JAY WILLIAMS

ILLUSTRATED BY IMERO GOBBATO

Parents' Magazine Press   New York

for my grandson, Ben

There are many nice things about being a king. But there is one very bad thing. That is, that it is very hard to find a job if you are out of work.

All that a king can do is rule. And if you have no kingdom, then you are out of work. That is what happened to young King Zar.

He was a good king, but he was young and without much experience. A bold, strong king with many soldiers attacked his kingdom. When the battle had ended, the strong king had won and young Zar found himself with no country, with no palace or house or hut. The strong king had even taken his crown. Zar

had twelve gold pieces, a suit of clothes, and a sword. So he set out to find work.

The road was long and the world was wide. He went to many lands, but no one wanted to hire a king without a kingdom. He had never known what it was to be hungry or thirsty or tired before, but now he learned.

Fortunately, as a king, Zar had already learned how to meet happiness or unhappiness with the same cheerful smile.

One day, his road led him through a thick forest. As he walked along thinking of this and that, he heard a small voice crying, "Pull me out! Oh, please pull me out!"

He looked about him. There, in a log, an ax was stuck fast. And the small voice seemed to be coming from its blade.

Zar took hold of the handle and with a twist, freed the ax.

At once, it turned into a man. He had a sharp face and shining hair the color of steel.

"Many thanks, stranger," he said. "I was cutting wood for a fire when my blade hit a tough knot, and there I stuck."

"But if you can turn yourself into a man, why didn't you do so?" asked Zar. "Then you could have freed yourself."

"Not at all," said the other, "for my nose would have been caught firmly in the log. I am grateful to you. Tell me who you are and where you are going."

Zar told his story.

"You are a king after my own heart," said the other, whose name was Edge. "I will join you and help you seek your fortune."

Off they went together. When nightfall came, Edge turned himself into an ax, cut wood, and they had a fine fire at which to eat their bread and cheese.

The next day, as they went along the dusty road, Zar heard a great bellowing. He turned aside to look. There, backed up against a rock, stood an elephant. Its trunk was raised in fright. A white-footed mouse scampered in the grass before it.

Zar took pity on the huge beast. He scooped up the mouse in his hat, carried it away, and let it go at a distance. When he returned, the elephant had turned into a large, lumbersome man with thick skin, large ears, and little pig-eyes.

"Many thanks, stranger," said the man. "Tiny things like mice give me the shivers. I was paralyzed with fear at the sight of that one."

"But," said Zar, "if you can turn yourself into a man, why didn't you do so? Then you could have chased off the mouse."

"Ah, but when I am a man I am just as frightened of mice as when I am an elephant," replied the man. "Now tell me who you are and where you are going."

Zar explained.

"Splendid!" said the man, whose name was Agus. "You're just the fellow for me. I'll go with you and help you find a job."

They went on, all three, and after a bit it began to rain. They took shelter under some trees, and all at once Zar heard a small, crackling voice crying, "Help, help!"

Looking around, he spied a fire burning with much smoke and smolder. The voice came from its center. Zar took off his cloak, and he held one end of it while Agus held the other. They stretched it over the fire and sheltered it from the rain. Soon it had blazed up brightly once more.

When it had done so, it turned into a man with bright red hair and freckles like sparks.

"Many thanks, strangers," he cried, snapping his fingers. "I thought I was done for."

"But if you can turn yourself into a man," said Zar, "why did you not do so? Then you could have taken shelter from the rain."

"Ah," said the other, whose name was Kindle, "but the rain came suddenly and weakened me so that I had no strength left.

Now tell me who you are and where you are going."

When he had heard Zar's story, he cried, "Good! I will join you and your companions, for it is sad to travel without friends in the world."

They all four marched on together, and now they never lacked for warmth or a cooking fire.

One evening, as they were making their camp, Zar heard a hissing like that of a hundred tea kettles boiling. He went to look, and his friends came with him. They found a huge black serpent with its tail tied into a knot. It writhed helplessly, trying to untangle itself.

Zar stepped forward, although Edge said, "Leave it alone. If you go too close, it may swallow you up or crush you in its coils."

But Zar had a soft heart. He bent over the serpent and with all his strength untied the knot. At once, the serpent turned into a man, tall, slender, and with a dark and shining skin.

"Many thanks, stranger," he said in a soft voice. "I tied that knot in my tail out of pride, to see if it could be done, and then I could not undo it."

"But if you can turn yourself into a man," said Zar, "why didn't you do so? Then you could have untied yourself."

"Do you think so?" smiled the other, whose name was Eryx. "Can you imagine what it would be like to have your legs tied into a knot? But come, tell me who you are and where you are going."

Zar did so.

"Excellent!" said Eryx. "I have been looking for someone to travel with, for the road has been long and lonely."

Then they all went on together in great friendship.

Before long, they came to the top of a high hill. There, among small trees, stood a taller, mightier one. As they rested beneath it, looking at the valley below, a sighing voice came from the tree. "Alas," it said, "oh glum and woesome woe."

Zar stood close to its bark. "Is there someone in trouble?" he asked.

"Look up into my branches," said the voice. "Do you see those nests? There are four of them, and all are filled with baby birds which cry and scream all day and night so that I never get any rest. If only I could be free of them!"

Zar climbed the tree. Carefully, he lifted down the four nests. With the help of his companions, he placed the nests in four smaller trees, while the parent birds flew anxiously about to make certain all was well.

When this was done, the tree turned into a dignified-looking man, whose hair and beard were as shaggy as moss.

"Many thanks, strangers," he said, in a slow, deep voice. "You cannot know what a relief it is to be rid of those noisy birds."

"But," said Zar, "if you can turn yourself into a man, why didn't you do so? Then you could have disposed of the nests yourself."

"Not so," replied the other, whose name was Furze, "for the instant I became a man, the nests would have fallen and the young birds would have been killed. I am much too kind to let such a thing happen. But tell me who you are and where you are going."

Zar obliged.

"That is good," said Furze. "You seem to me to be a fine sort of man, king or no king. I will go with you and help you find your fortune, for if two heads are better than one, six are better yet."

They all took the road down the hill and into the broad valley. At the edge of a wood they paused, for they heard a loud and angry humming, mixed with snarls.

"It sounds," said Agus, "like trouble. Let us take another road." For in spite of his size, he was rather timid.

But Zar strode forward to see what was happening.

He found that a brown bear was breaking its way into a honey tree. A swarm of bees buzzed about it, but the long thick fur of the bear protected it from the stings.

Zar drew his sword and ran at the bear. For a moment, it stood up to fight, but when it had been pricked once or twice by the sharp sword it turned tail and shambled away.

At once, the swarm of bees turned into a small, fat man with a beard the color of honey. Instead of a sting, he wore a long sword at his side.

"Many thanks, stranger," he said. "I feared I was about to lose all the honey I had saved for my own dinner."

"But if you can turn yourself into a man," said Zar, "why didn't you do so? Then you could have driven off the bear with your own sword."

The other, whose name was Dumble, scratched his head. He was, in fact, not very bright.

"I never thought of that," he said. "But tell me who you are and where you are going."

When Zar had done so, Dumble said, "Huzzah! I'll go along with you, and when you have found your fortune you can build me a hive where there are no bears."

So away they went, all seven, and now they had plenty of honey to spread on their bread, and the way was made easy with their joking and storytelling.

They came, at length, to a fine city with towers and banners and a beautiful palace, lining the banks of a busy river. They

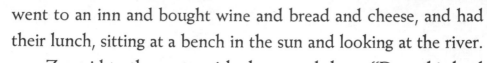

went to an inn and bought wine and bread and cheese, and had their lunch, sitting at a bench in the sun and looking at the river.

Zar said to the pretty girl who served them, "Does this land have a king?"

"Oh, yes," she answered, "and he is not a bad one, either. But he is having a certain amount of trouble these days, for he has only one child, a daughter, and he cannot find a husband for her."

"Is she so ugly?" Zar asked.

"Ugly? She is as lovely as a spring morning after a hard

winter. She is so fair that flowers close enviously at the sight of her."

"Then why can't she find a husband?"

"Because," said the girl, "her father has but one fault, he is terribly proud. He has sworn that his daughter shall marry none but a king, and unfortunately all the kings hereabouts are married already."

"Ah," said Zar, "then perhaps he is in luck—and so am I."

He paid the girl, and gave her a kiss of thanks. Then he and his six friends went up to the palace.

There, they were brought before the king, whose name was Invictus XV, the Ever-Glorious. He was a thin, worried-looking man with the bad habit of biting his nails in spite of his magnificent name. Aside from this, however, he was very royal. When he heard Zar's name, he came down from the throne and greeted him in a kindly way.

"I knew your father," he said. "And I was very distressed to hear of your misfortunes. So now you are out of a job?"

"Exactly," said Zar. "The kingdoms I have visited, already have rulers. But there is another job I am fit for. I will make a good husband for a princess."

King Invictus stroked his beard. "That may be so," he said. "However, you must admit there are problems. A king with no kingdom is not much of a match. And my daughter is very rich."

"When I marry her, I will be rich, too," Zar pointed out.

"There is certainly some truth to that," admitted King Invictus. "But I think you will agree that in this case we must use the

old-fashioned method to find out whether you are worthy. I intend to set you three tests. If you can pass them, you may marry my daughter."

Zar nodded thoughtfully. "First," said he, "let me see your daughter."

King Invictus sent a servant to fetch her. In a few moments, she entered the room. When she came in, it was as though hundreds of birds had begun to sing, or as if the sun had burst through

clouds. Zar was dazzled, and behind him, Dumble was so over-
come that he fainted dead away and Eryx had to fan him with
his hat.

As for the princess, she looked straight at Zar and her eyes
lighted like stars.

"Very well," Zar stammered, turning to King Invictus. "I
accept the tests. Let them begin at once. I ask only one thing."

"Ask away," said King Invictus.

"No king does everything for himself, as you well know,"
Zar said. "We all have councilors, generals, ministers, and servants
to help us. So you must allow me to call upon my six friends to
aid me in the tests."

King Invictus nodded. "I agree," he said. "But remember that
if you fail in any of them, you and your six companions will lose
your heads."

Zar and his companions were led by the king's steward into

a large chamber. It had seven walls and seven windows. Under each window was a long table, and each table was heaped high with food. Next to each table was a huge vat containing seven gallons of wine.

"This," said the steward, "is the Feast Fit For a King. It is King Invictus' wish that you should eat and drink everything in this room. All must be gone in the space of one hour, and nothing must be left, for no one may turn away unsatisfied from the dinner of a king."

He left them. And for a while, Zar stared at all the food and drink and rubbed his chin.

"I'm sure we are all hungry," he said, "but there is enough food here for a town full of people."

"Perhaps," said Furze, in his sober way, "we ought to climb out of the windows and escape. There is one window for each of us."

Zar shook his head. He turned to Kindle. "Become a fire," he said.

At once, Kindle turned into flames. Darting about the room, he went from dish to dish, from platter to platter, and everything he touched was consumed, devoured, burned to the finest ash, and then to nothing.

Zar said to Agus, "Become an elephant."

Agus did so. Dipping his trunk into the vats, one after the other, he sucked up the wine. He swelled until he was twice as large as before, and he swayed with dizziness, but when he was done every drop had vanished.

Then both Agus and Kindle turned into men once more.

At the end of an hour, the steward returned. His eyes opened wide at the empty plates and the empty vats.

All he said, however, was, "Follow me."

He led them out of the castle, out of the city, and high into the hills. The land grew barren and wild, and a bitter wind blew over the rocks.

"Now," said the steward, "it is King Invictus' wish that you should fetch him the golden egg of the Eagle of the Heights."

"Where is this egg?" asked Zar.

The steward pointed ahead. "Continue on this path," he said, "and you will come to a gap in the earth. On the other side, there is a cliff, and on the top of the cliff is a casket. The egg is in the casket. When you have it, bring it back to the castle. As for me, if you will excuse me, I am feeling the chill."

He bowed, and went home to make himself a hot drink.

"It all sounds easy enough," said Eryx.

The seven friends followed the path. It wound higher, and at last ended at the brink of a wide and deep gap. It was too wide to jump, and far below were sharp rocks like the teeth in a wolf's mouth.

"Well," said Kindle, briskly, "all we need is plenty of wood, saws, hammers, and nails, and we can build a bridge."

"A bridge we shall have," said Zar, "but we will not build it." And turning to Eryx, he said, "Become a serpent."

At once, Eryx turned into a huge serpent. Coiling the tip of his tail several times around a rock, he drew back his great body

and then shot himself forward across the gap. He seized a gnarled tree on the other side with his teeth, and held tight.

One by one, the others ran across his body as on a narrow bridge.

"Wait here," said Zar, "for I hope we shall all come back again."

Before them, there now rose a cliff. It was like the straight wall of a house, and as smooth as glass. It was not very high, but it had no need to be, for there was no way to climb it.

Zar said to Furze, "Become a tree."

Furze set his long feet firmly on the ground next to the cliff. His shape changed, and there stood a tall tree, its branches making a ladder up the face of the cliff.

Swiftly, Zar climbed it. At the top of the cliff, he found a little chest. Snatching it up, he climbed down again. Furze became a man once more.

Zar examined the chest. But it seemed to be all of one piece: there was no lid, no handle, no keyhole, and no key.

He said to Edge, "Become an ax."

At once, Edge was a gleaming ax. He leaped into the air and fell with a smash upon the chest. It burst open, and from it rolled a shining golden egg.

Zar tucked the egg safely away in his pocket. Then he and the others crossed the gap again over Eryx. Eryx drew himself slowly back, coil upon coil, until he had rejoined them, and then he became a man. He rubbed his ribs and groaned.

"Some of you have heavy boots," he complained.

They returned to the city. They entered the throne room of the palace, and Zar laid the golden egg in the hands of King Invictus.

"Good," said the king. "There is but one thing more. You were driven from your kingdom, my boy, and now you must show me that you have learned to defend yourself."

He clapped his hands. From the sides of the room sprang soldiers, each with fierce moustaches, each bearing a huge two-handed sword. They advanced on Zar and his friends.

"Dumble!" cried Zar. "Become a swarm of bees!"

And in the wink of an eye, Dumble vanished and in his place rose a dark, angry cloud of bees. They flew straight at the soldiers' faces, and from the soldiers came yells of anguish, of sorrow, and of despair. Turning, they fled away, some of them jumping from the windows, others hiding in the cellars, and others diving into the royal fishpond. The battle was over.

When Dumble had taken a man's shape again, King Invictus XV, the Ever-Glorious, rubbing a sting from a stray bee, said, "King Zar, the tests have been passed. You have proved your right to my daughter's hand. The princess is yours."

They all cheered. Nobles and ladies filled the throne room and hailed young Zar, who would some day be their king. The princess was brought, and she and Zar kissed each other as the sound of all the bells in the city filled the air.

A great banquet was held, and in the places of honor, beside

the two kings and the princess, sat Zar's six companions, now made lords of the land.

"There's just one thing about the whole story which I don't understand," said the king's steward, who was sitting at the table next to Agus. "Each of you six had something he could do best. It seems to me that it was you who passed the tests, not Zar. What did he do?"

Agus smiled an elephant smile, his small eyes twinkling.

"He did what only a good king can do," he replied. "He led us."